MAMA REX AND T

Shop for Shoes

by Rachel Vail

illustrations by Steve Björkman

SCHOLASTIC INC.
New York Toronto London Auckland Sydney
Mexico City New Delhi Hong Kong

For Liam,
not yet in shoes;
you make me feel happy.

ISBN 0-439-19919-0

Text copyright © 2000 by Rachel Vail.
Art copyright © 2000 by Steve Björkman.

All rights reserved. Published by Scholastic Inc.
SCHOLASTIC and associated logos are trademarks and/or
registered trademarks of Scholastic Inc.

12 11 10 9 8 7 6 5 4 3 2   0 1 2 3 4 5 6/0

Book Design by Cristina Costantino

Printed in the U.S.A.
First Scholastic printing, November 2000

Contents

Chapter 1
OLD SHOES

On their way home from the playground, Mama Rex looked at T's shoes. "You need new shoes," said Mama Rex.

T looked down at his shoes. He watched them swing into view one at a time, beneath him on the sidewalk.

"I like these shoes," said T. "What's wrong with these shoes?"

"There are holes in the toes," said Mama Rex.

"My toes like fresh air," said T.

"The sole is peeling off the bottom of that one," said Mama Rex.

"I like the flapping noise it makes," said T.

"They are filthy dirty," said Mama Rex.

"That's because they are always on the ground," said T.

"That's true," said Mama Rex.

T picked up a perfect round rock from the sidewalk and put it in his pocket.

It was for his collection. He had a jar on his shelf half-full of perfect round rocks.

"How do they feel?" Mama Rex asked.

"Who?" asked T.

"Your shoes," said Mama Rex.

T thought about that.

He had never thought about how his shoes felt before.

Mama Rex and T crossed the street. T was still thinking.

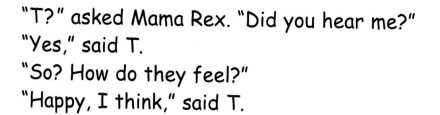

"T?" asked Mama Rex. "Did you hear me?"
"Yes," said T.
"So? How do they feel?"
"Happy, I think," said T.

Mama Rex stopped walking. She looked at T.
T thought some more.
"Maybe they feel bored sometimes," said T.
"When they're in my closet."

Mama Rex smiled at T. She knelt down in front of him and held both his hands.

"I meant, how do they feel to you? How do they feel on your feet?"

"Oh," said T. "You meant, how do my feet feel?"

"Yes," said Mama Rex. She smiled at T. "That's what I meant."

T thought about that.

He wiggled his toes around and rocked from one foot to the other. He imagined being his feet.

T lay down on the sidewalk and looked up, to see things the way his feet did. The buildings looked very tall. The sky was brighter blue in the middle and lighter on the edges. The sidewalk had sparkles on it and was cool. There was a humming sort of noise.

"My feet feel happy, too," said T. "They had fun in the playground."

Mama Rex stood up. "Fine," she said.
"Happy," said T. "But a little tiny bit squished."
"You need new shoes," said Mama Rex.
"I know," said T.

Chapter 2
THE SHOE STORE

Mama Rex and T walked to the shoe store.
There were balloons tied to the door.
T loved balloons. He hoped he would get one.

Inside the shoe store there were kids everywhere. Kids were standing on seats, tugging on grown-ups. Kids were crawling under seats, hiding with their bottoms in the air. Babies were tied into their strollers, screaming and sweating.

Mama Rex wrote down T's name on a paper
attached to a clipboard.

T looked at his name on the paper. It was next
to number twenty-seven.

"Twenty-seven is a high number," said T.

T sat down on a bench to wait.

"Mommy!" screamed a boy. "That dinosaur is
sitting in my seat!"

T stood up. He didn't want to lose his chance at a balloon by fighting. He leaned against a wall to wait.

A boot fell off the wall. T tried to catch it. He swung around and opened his arms. T's tail knocked some party shoes off the wall. T tried to catch the party shoes. He was clonked in the nose by a pair of galoshes. T fell on the floor under snow boots and sandals and galoshes.

"Twenty-one," called out the shoe store lady. "Ezekiel?"

The bench boy jumped up. He was number twenty-one. His name was Ezekiel.

T was happy he was not number twenty-one, Ezekiel.

He was busy balancing shoes on the plastic shelves sticking out of the wall. He wanted to hurry, so he'd still have a chance at a balloon.

Mama Rex tried to help him but she had a
different style. She put a shiny black shoe with
a strappy red sandal and a fuzzy brown boot.

"I like it by color," said T, moving the strappy
red sandal next to a clumpy red high-top. "And it's
friendlier if they face each other," he explained.

"There's a snow boot on your tail," whispered Mama Rex.

T looked at his tail. Mama Rex was right.

T thought the snow boot looked nice upside down. He put it on the shelf that way.

Turns out snow boots have trouble balancing upside down.

"Twenty-seven," said the shoe store lady with the glasses necklace. "T?"

T raised his small arm.

"Your name is T?" the shoe store lady asked. "Just T?"

"Yes," said T, wishing his name were something bigger, like Ezekiel.

The shoe store lady smiled. "My name is B," she said.

"Just B?" asked T.

"Yes," she said.

"I like your necklace," said T.

B asked Mama Rex and T to sit down. She took T's ankle in her hand and looked at T's old shoe. "I like your shoes," she said.

"Me, too," said T.

"He needs some a little bigger," said Mama Rex.

B gently pulled the old shoe off T's foot and placed T's foot down on a cold metal foot measurer. "Stand up, please," she said, and after T stood up, she said, "Hmm."

She flipped the foot measurer around and gently pulled off T's other shoe. She picked up her glasses on their lanyard chain and looked at T's feet.

"Your feet have grown," she said.

"Yes," said Mama Rex. "They match the rest of him."

B looked at the rest of T. "So they do," she said.

B took off her glasses and walked toward the back of the shoe store. She disappeared behind a gold curtain.

B came back with four boxes. She opened them one at a time, like presents.

T looked at Mama Rex, to see which he was supposed to choose.

"It's up to you," said Mama Rex.

T pointed at the red high-top sneakers.

B loosened the laces and slipped them onto his feet.

T walked around the shoe store. He ran. He jumped. He came back to the chair and sat down.

"So?" asked B.

"I like them," said T.

"How do your feet feel?" asked Mama Rex.

"Good," said T. "But a little pinchy."

"Maybe you should try another pair," said Mama Rex.

"Good idea," said T.

In the black loafers, his feet felt good but a
little slippy.

In the white running shoes, they felt good but
a little boingy.

In the brown work boots, they felt good.

"But?" asked Mama Rex.

"But?" asked B.

"Just good," said T.

Chapter 3
NEW SHOES

B placed T's old shoes into the box. She stood up and looked at the wall.

"Who rearranged my shoe wall?" she asked.

"I did," admitted T.

Twenty-one Ezekiel was leaving the shoe store with a balloon tied to his wrist.

"I'm sorry," said T.

"The wall looks good this way," said B.

"You think so?" asked T.

"Much friendlier," said B.

T smiled.

B carried the box above her head, through the crowd, to the cash register.

Mama Rex followed B.

T followed Mama Rex, watching his new work boots meet the rug beneath them.

Mama Rex paid.

T practiced some small jumps.

"Thank you, Mama Rex," said T.

"You're welcome, T," said Mama Rex.

They opened the door and left the noisy shoe
store. T carried the bag that held his old shoes.

Outside it was a little darker than when they
went in and a little cooler.

"This is the sidewalk," T said to his new work
boots.

"Wait!" yelled the shoe store lady whose name
was just B.

Mama Rex and T turned around.

B had a balloon in her hand. She tied it around T's wrist.

"I hope you like yellow," she whispered.

"I love yellow," said T. "Thank you."

T looked up at his balloon, floating yellow against the blue sky.

"How do the new shoes feel?" asked B.

T looked down at his new work boots and then up at Mama Rex.

"I think they feel happy," he said.